Not Safe For
Kids

An Illustrated Children's Book
For Adults

Written by Kevin Shamel and Illustrated by Jim Agpalza

SPUNK GOBLIN PRESS

"YOU CAN MAKE A QUICK TRICK CHICK STACK." —Dr. Seuss

SPUNK GOBLIN PRESS

AN IMPRINT OF ERASERHEAD PRESS

ERASERHEAD PRESS
P.O. BOX 10065
PORTLAND, OR 97296

WWW.ERASERHEADPRESS.COM

ISBN: 978-1-62105-219-7

FOR THE MOST FUN, READ THIS BOOK ALOUD, **AS IF TO A PACK OF IDIOT CHILDREN**.

Being in the company of children subjects a person to a vast array of fears, complicated questions, strange assumptions and apprehensions about society, life, death, and one's place in this weird world. This allows the opportunity to really fuck people up for life. Which, while usually a lot of fun, can sometimes end in disaster for everyone else around the little shits. The author and artist believe it is best to be purposeful in this endeavor and not just fuck people up willy-nilly.

Not being around kids is pretty nice, but you can only live vicariously through parents and caretakers to experience the joys of molding an innocent little human into a shuddering wreck of a person. Unless you go out of your way to mess with other people's kids. Which **is** fun, but puts you near those creepy little snot-factories.

The author and artist (blessed parents each) bring this book to you in the co-creative spirit of extended family, whether or not you have access to these little blank psychological canvases. They believe that everyone should have a fair shake in destroying futures and confirming fears, be it parents or child-hating zero populationists and hipsters. If you don't mind being arrested, find some kids and have yourself a reading circle. Or don't. Because fuck them—if they're too stupid to read it themselves, they don't deserve to even look at the pictures.

Tucking You In

Yes. There *are* monsters under your bed.

Well, they're in a room below your floor, but the invisible trapdoor that **leads** to the room is under your bed.

Oh, yeah. They're ***totally*** dangerous.

For one thing, they like to eat any part of a kid that hangs over the bed. So like, if your arm dangled over, and the monsters happened to come out and see it, they'd just snap it off with their rows of needle-teeth. You'd wake up screaming, with blood shooting out of the stump at the end of your arm, spraying all over the wall and your face. Your bones would be jutting out of ripped-up flesh and muscle. It would hurt ***so much***. And to shut you up, the monster would jump out and tear off your head, or rip out your throat, or just mash-in your face. They **HATE** screaming.

That's **one** thing that makes them dangerous.

But now it's time to sleep. I'll tell you more about the monsters tomorrow, as long as you don't piss them off tonight.

Oh. They hate farts, too. So try not to fart while you sleep. Or snore.

And *pray* that your nightlight doesn't burn out, because that's really **the only thing keeping them from opening the door** under your bed.

G'night. I love you.

Wouldn't it be **cool** if you could go back in time and fight the *dinosaurs* for control of the moon?

No, it wouldn't be. **You'd totally die.**

Stupid.

Running Fast Enough to Fly

Did you know that holding babies makes you **run faster**?

Try it and see!

The next time someone has a baby, ask if you can hold it. The moment you have it in your arms, *take off running.*

The more people who chase you, the *faster you can run.*

If you can get ten people running after you, you can fly. *Try* to not drop the baby, but once you leave the ground it doesn't matter.

You'll be able to fly without it.

Kevin Shamel & Jim Agpalza

Birth

Do you remember when you were first born and you had to cut your way out of your **real mom**, and she died and was replaced by a robot that is exactly like your real mom except she's a *robot* who sneaks into your room at night and sucks some of your life out of you when you're sleeping?

Of course you don't. All babies have their memories erased when they're nine months old after they've been milked for all their **sad-juice** and had their stomach-knives removed and all that's left is a belly stump, which doctors tie-off like the end of a balloon and let ants eat down to the knot.

Do you know that you would live to be **three hundred years-old** if your life wasn't slowly sucked away by your robot mom? You would.

Do you know that if your dad is around when it's time for you to be born that **HE** is killed and replaced by a robot that is exactly like him, but is *a robot*, too? Yes.

That's why the only *REAL* old men are the ones who abandoned their pregnant girlfriends or wives or one-night-stands, or cousins who slipped drugs in their beer on the 4th of July and took them out on a boat and told them that **the sea serpent** was about to eat them and the only way to stop it was to have sex, even though they were *cousins* (which happens more than you'd expect). All other fathers are robots.

Grandfathers are ***double robots***. So are grandmothers. Great grandparents do not actually exist. If someone tells you that they have living great-grandparents, they are fucking liars and you should kick them in the genitals and never speak to them again.

No one knows how long the robots have been in charge of us, but it really doesn't matter. The only way to stop them would be for everyone to **kill their parents...**

Work Isn't Real

Did you know that **"work"** isn't real? When your parents say that they are going there, they are really going to the coolest water park in the world—*a secret one where kids aren't allowed.*

It has chicks in bikinis, muscle-dudes who only wear *Speedos*, an underwater candy store, a chocolate pool (with fountain), six bars, **free weed**, giant fish bowls with huge-ass fish and treasure chests for scuba diving, three magic shows a day, naked aquatic ballet, sixteen super waterslides, fifteen *semi*-super waterslides, two shipwrecks, talking dolphins, Aquaman, **a friendly shark**, live music, horse surfing and the Former Child-Star Swim Team.

You know how when your parents come home from "work", they always look kinda tired and they tease you and ignore your answer about how school was and force you to eat **canned beets**? That's because they've partied all day and had more fun than you have *ever* had, and they kinda want to rub it in your face without you even knowing.

Kevin Shamel & Jim Agpalza
Exploring
the Natural World

What most kids worry about when they climb trees is falling out. But that is a stupid thing to be scared of. What they should worry about is being **EATEN** by the tree. What most kids don't realize is that *trees eat children.* You know how their leaves are always blowing in the wind, and they whisper and stuff? That's to lure you into climbing them. Then their branches wrap around you like really strong arms or **mean spaghetti**, and long narrow mouths open up and down their trunk (they have *hundreds* of mouths) and their splintery jagged teeth rip you to shreds while stuffing you inside.

Picking flowers is bad, too. Because when you do, poison seeps out of their stems and gets sucked right through your skin and you start to get **old.**

Be careful of rocks, also. They just *pretend* they can't move and don't eat people. They totally can, and they totally do. Even the little ones. **How do you think they get big**?

You know how people say that bee-stings cure AIDS? Those people obviously haven't been stung by a **stupid bee**. That hurts! It's not worth it. Dumbasses. Besides, it's wasp-stings that don't hurt and cure everything wrong with you. **Even ugliness.** Don't believe me? Try it out. First hit a beehive with a stick and let some bees sting you. You'll find out that it hurts. Then *go poke a wasp nest* so you can be cured by their painless stings. Take an ugly friend with you to make him or her beautiful! If you *are* the ugly friend, **good for you**!

Sorry, Kid

Does your *poop* smell bad?

Does your mom and dad's poop smell bad?

If so, then you are **dying.** And they are dying.

Anyone whose poop doesn't smell like flowers, candy, moss, a glacial wind, puppy breath, peanut butter, or popcorn is dying.

You will probably die tomorrow.

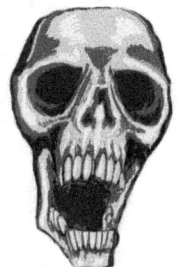

Your parents might already be dead.

You should go and check *right now*.

If it sounds like they are wrestling, you should run to the neighbors' houses and bring as many people as you can into your parents' room as quietly as possible to be sure they are okay. If you have a video camera, you should film everything and put it on **YouTube** before you die.

There's no way to save yourself after your poop starts smelling bad. So don't even *think* of figuring out how to survive this. It sucks, but that's the way it is.

Think of the starving kids in Africa
before you start whining.

Kevin Shamel & Jim Agpalza

BABBLE

You know how people all speak a bunch of different languages, and you can never know if they're saying something bad about you?

You should just always assume that they are.

I heard that the reason people speak other stupid languages is because a long time ago, Jesus got all mad at everyone for building a tower and he used his powers to turn into Godzilla and smashed the tower down and made everyone speak Chinese.

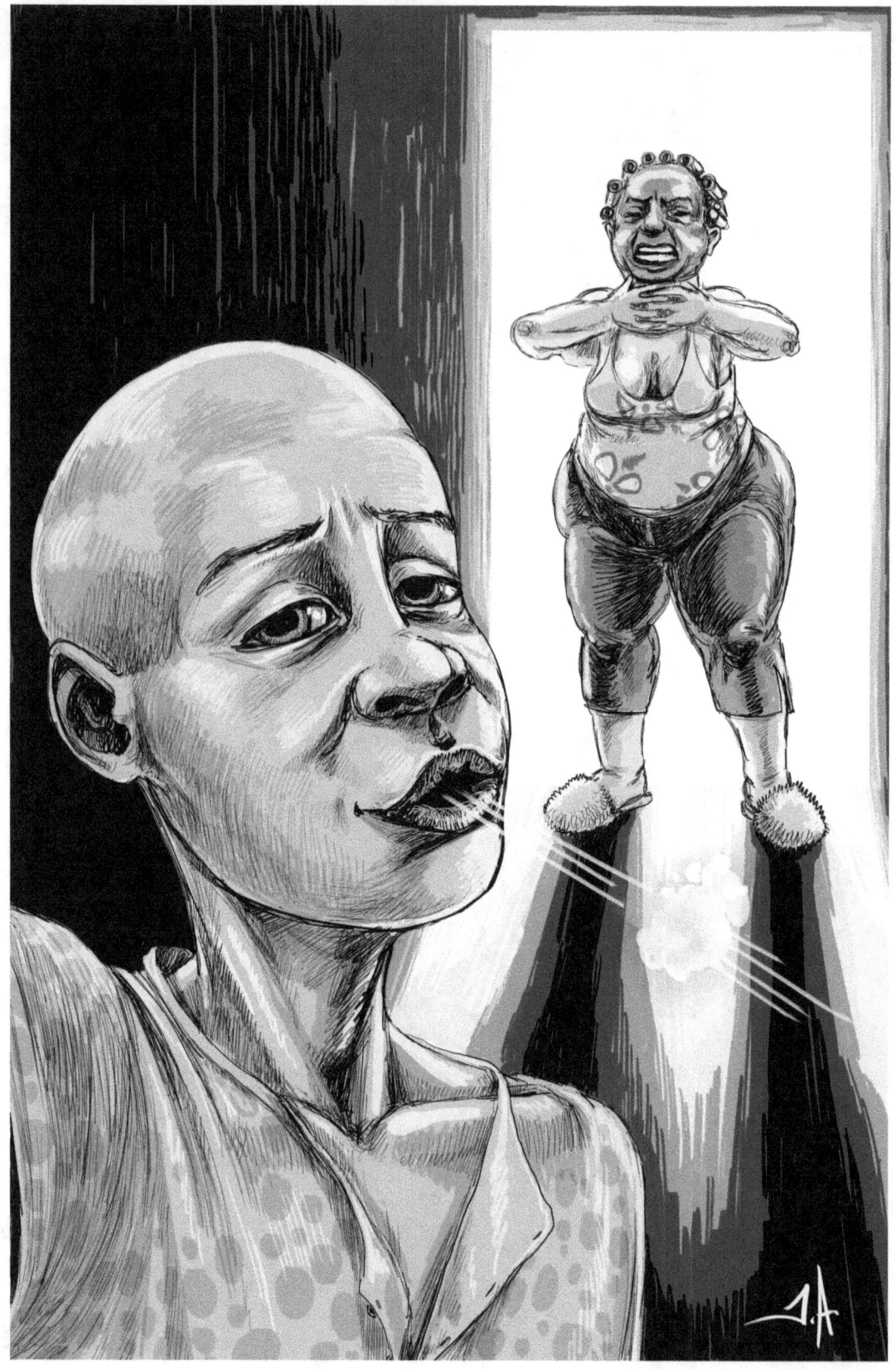

Do you count how many breaths you take in a day?

You should only take *twenty-thousand and forty-three* breaths a day.

If you take more, someone in the world dies from not being able to breathe.

You don't want it to be your **mom**, do you?

Kevin Shamel & Jim Agpalza

Anatomy

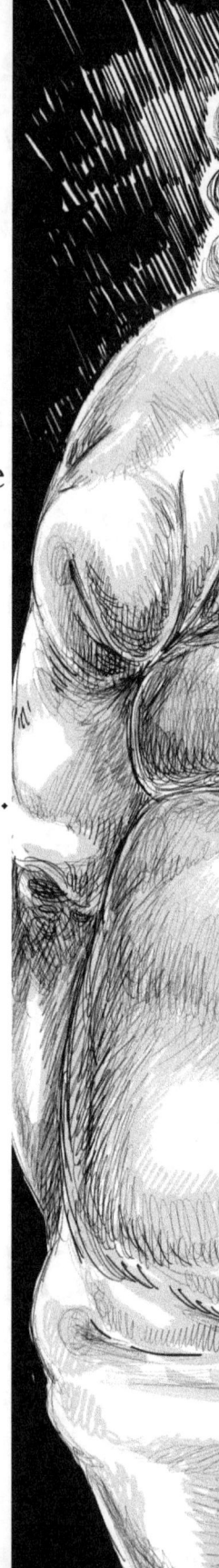

Your skeleton **hates** you.

It's stuck inside you, and it wants out. That's why you grow. It's just stretching and stretching you. One day it will tear free.

That's why old people are *floppy*. Their bones are gone. If you look at an old person naked (which you really **REALLY** don't want to do), you'll see the scar up their back where their skeleton escaped.

It hurts a lot, too. That's what makes old people mean. It's also why they pretend to be nice to you. They want to steal your **skeleton**.

Never fall for your Granny's bullshit when she's feeding you cookies or letting you win at videogames. She's just waiting for you to fall asleep so she can **cut out your bones** and stand up straight again.

That never works, though every single old person tries it, because your skeleton just wants to be free. Once it is, it will kill anyone who stands in its way of escaping to *Skeleton Island*. Especially old people.

Because they are weak.

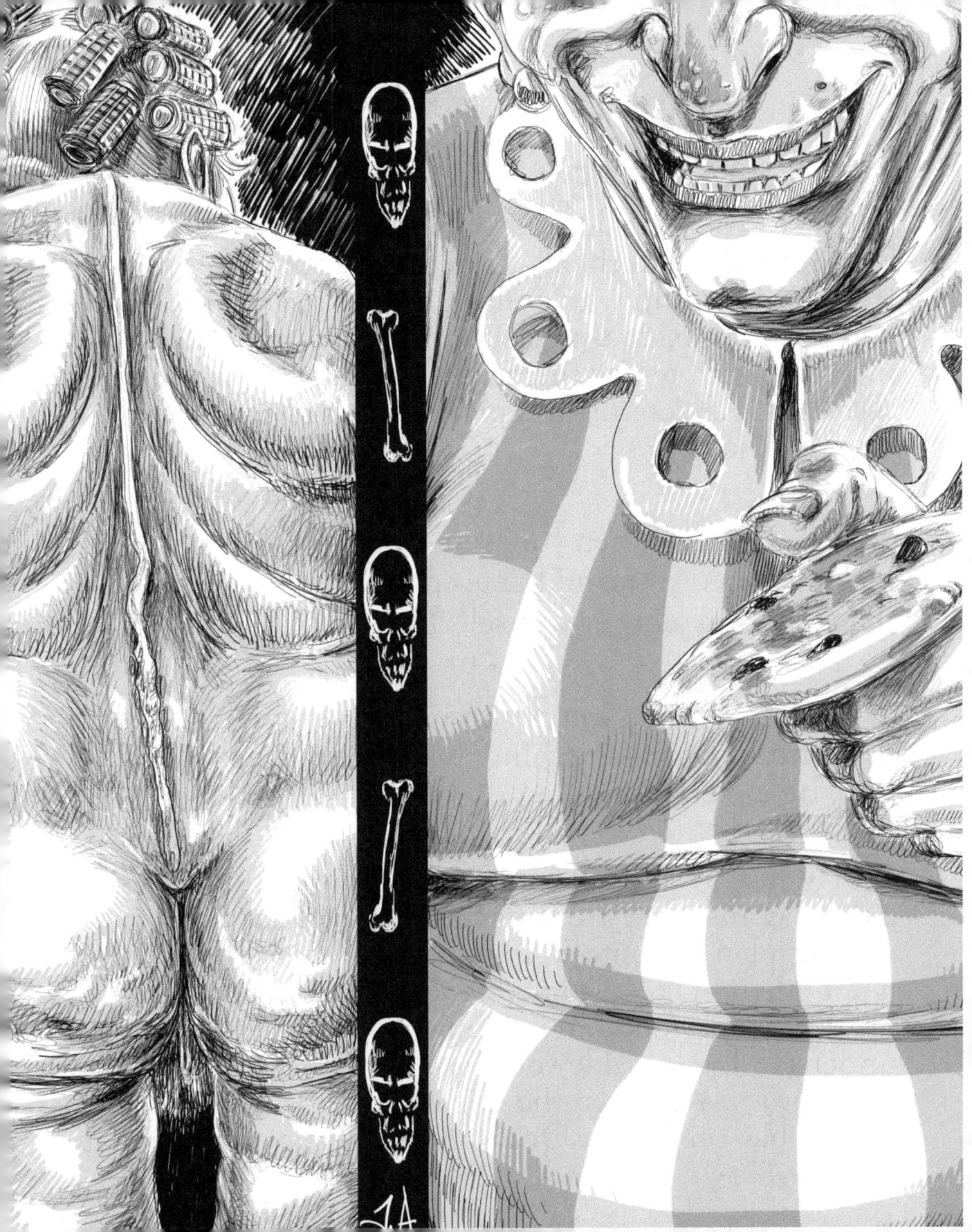

Kevin Shamel & Jim Agpalza

Things You Might Want to Consider

Chainsaw rides: Sit on a running chainsaw on top of a steep hill with the blade between your legs. Reach your hand back behind you, pull the trigger to start the blade, and push off. **Ride that chainsaw down that hill!** It's WAY more fun with ten or fifteen friends all lined up on their own saws. Rev 'em up and pick up your feet, **it's a wild downhill jam**.

Remember when you were a baby? You were so fucking stupid you couldn't even talk and you just laid there and shit all over yourself. **Ha!** *Stupid.*

The first time you get hit by a car it doesn't hurt. It's like a free pass or something. Just once, though, so after that, **be careful**.

When people tell you not to feed something, it's either because they are stingy assholes or have some devious plan to incite eating disorders. You should ignore them. Like, if someone says, "Please don't feed my dog people-food." You should nod your head like you understand, but inside you should think, *Fuck you, you dog-depriving jerk*, And feed the dog whatever you can as soon as possible, on the sly. Or if there's a sign at the zoo that

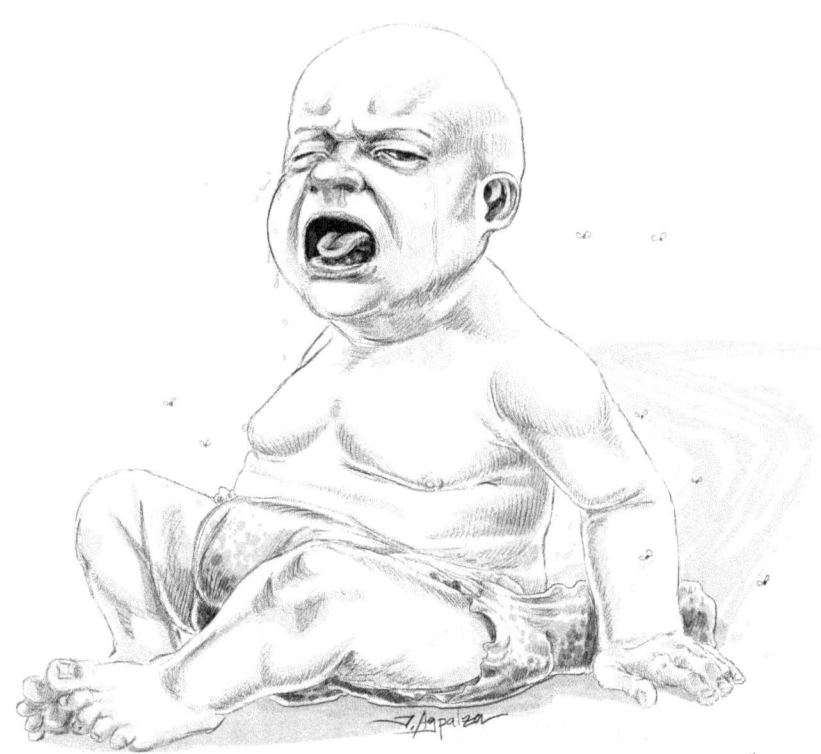

says, **"Don't Feed the Lions"**, it's because zookeepers hate animals and secretly starve them to death. You should throw the nearest hotdog, sno-cone, or baby through the bars the moment no one is looking. And if you're in a National Park, like Yellowstone, and there are pamphlets, and signs, and the person at the gate says it, and there's sky-writing about it, and all the rangers' trucks have bumper stickers saying, *don't feed the animals*, you should totally not only ignore it, and especially feed the bears that will come right up to your car, but also report that shit to the **President** when you get home. Email that jerk.

All that stuff about not looking directly at a solar-eclipse is old wives' tales. Same thing about crystal meth being bad for you, and how brushing your teeth matters—it doesn't. **Don't bother.**

You know how the moon follows you? If not, check it out. Walk around some night when you can see it. It will follow you wherever you go. It does that because it's **stalking you**. If you look away from it long enough, it'll snatch you up. You can't breathe on the moon. Just sayin'.

Santa Claus isn't real. If your parents haven't told you that, it's because they're either **sadistic liars** or conformist robots—in either case, they don't love you.

Don't tell them you know, though. Just start asking only for outrageous shit at Christmastime like boats, **Space Camp**, stained-glass dildos, diamonds made from their ashes, and reindeer steaks. Play that shit up, and if you get stupid crap for Christmas, act enraged and start a campaign to wipe out the North Pole. Tell your parents that you're friends with some hackers from **Anonymous** and they're using your parents' bank accounts to fund *"The Attack"*. Tell them you just ordered guns from a guy in Istanbul.

While we're being honest, the Easter Bunny and the Tooth Fairy are bullshit, too.

But Satan is REAL!!!!!

Have you ever had one of those dreams where you were *naked in public?*

Pervert.

Kevin Shamel & Jim Agpalza

Don't Try This at Home

When TV shows say, *"Don't try this at home!"* and then say it's because the stuff is dangerous or whatever, they're **lying**.

The reason is:

YOU are their competition.

OF COURSE you can track Bigfoot and contact ghosts better than them, or sneak into homes and make weapons from common household items, or train monkeys to attack your neighbors, or ride a tricycle off a stupid ramp while holding a bowling ball with your seat on **fire.**

Of COURSE you can rewire a building's electrical system, do wing-suit jumping, **shoot bottle-rockets out of your butt**, or rescue an injured wolf better than any douchebag on TV.

AND you'll get paid for it!

Aquaman

Did you know that you actually *can* breathe underwater? It's true. Your body doesn't really like it at first, but you totally can. Like a mermaid.

Here's how to do it:

Since your body will want to float, and also your instincts to fight your way to the surface for boring old air will kick-in, sometimes actually rendering you unconscious, where you'll float to the surface, roll on your back, and breathe. I know! **Stupid body.**

In order to stop this from happening, it's best to really weigh yourself down. Jumping from somewhere like a bridge or a pier into extra deep water is a good idea, especially if you can manage to do it when no one is around, so they don't fuck things up by trying to "save" you.

If you make yourself a *mermaid outfit* by wrapping your legs together with duct tape, it will make the experience that much more interesting. Like you're a fish-person, or a **horrible mutant kid** who crawled out of the basement of an abortion clinic. Or a mermaid. You can hop, that's no big deal.

It's best if you chain yourself to some cinderblocks, or an old refrigerator if you can manage. If your friends will help you, ***enlist their assist!*** It's cool to help-out your buddies.

Once you've been underwater for about a minute, or when you start feeling the pressure really building in your lungs, just breathe out as hard as you can. In the next moment, before you know it, you'll be breathing water!

This is when you'll be glad you're securely fastened to whatever heavy objects you've calculated will hold you on the bottom. A handy reference guide for underwater weight measurements can be found at any shipyard or bar near the docks. Just ask for the saltiest cock around, it's **sailor talk**.

Keep the keys to the locks securing your chains in your shoe, wrapped in seven plastic bags, each individually secured with zip-ties. Once you've gotten used to underwater breathing you'll want to free yourself from the fridge (or whatever's holding you down). Don't worry about accidentally floating *now*. And have fun exploring the bottom! You might find some coins or sea glass. Bring a spear gun to hunt sharks.

Good luck!

Kevin Shamel & Jim Agpalza

How to Win a Snowball Fight No Matter What

Use **rocks** instead of snowballs. Only suckers use snow. Make sure the rocks are hard and pointy. After the first volley, your enemies should either be in shock, trying to escape, or standing up in front of their forts, whining that you're using rocks. It's time for your second volley. *And perhaps a third.*

Once your enemies are unconscious or dead, you can steal the snowgear that their rich mommies and daddies bought them, even though their other stuff was perfectly good and they just *fucking threw it all away* and pretended that they drove the three blocks to Goodwill to donate it. You and your friends **know** because you went to Goodwill every day for the past week, since those assholes showed up talking shit about their lycra-lined poly-fibers, double-thick triple-woven wool and silk ski-masks, and brand new **baby panda boots**.

So now you've got all their stuff because they used snowballs like *dumbasses*. You can drag the unconscious ones into the street and cover them with snow for when the bus comes to really teach them a lesson in humility. Or in **something**, that's for sure.

I love wintertime, don't you?

Spoilers are *Bullshit*

Do you know that if you read the end of a book first, like, the last page or two, and then you start from the beginning again, that when you reach the ending, it will be *DIFFERENT?*

Yep.

It works on movies, too. Watch the last five or ten minutes first, and then watch from the beginning. It'll have a *different ending.*

It works for any recorded TV show as well.

Also, when people tell you not to "spoil the ending" it's because they're **stupid**, and they don't know that you can't. It will of course change once you tell them.

So feel free to just tell them anyway. If they try and do that thing where they put their fingers in their ears and yell, "La la la la! I CAN'T **HEAR** YOU!" punch them in the stomach.

They will move their hands away from their head automatically. If you hit them hard enough, and they're all curled-up on the ground, you can bend down and tell them the ending right in their **dumb fucking ear**.

Try it!

Kevin Shamel & Jim Agpalza

Submarine Wars!

One of the **coolest** things to use for a pretend submarine is an old refrigerator or freezer. Just make sure the door will still close. Usually only one kid can fit in a fridge, but if you're small, a couple of you can cram inside, just like real Navy seamen. Freezers are like *nuclear* subs—they're bigger and can hold more people. I have seen six children recovered from **ONE freezer** in a junk yard. They're roomy!

Old metal appliances are bulletproof, too. That makes them perfect for playing *Sub Attack*. Find a junkyard or old person's house with multiple abandoned appliances. Stoves won't work, so don't bother. Invite some of your older friends to try out your new shooting course at 4PM. You can paint **bulls-eyes** on your "submarines", before you and your friends jump inside and batten-down the hatches while you wait for the older kids to arrive.

If you're still awake when the shooting starts, you can all yell things at each other, like, "Fire torpedoes!" and "Starboard full-stop!" and **"Aaaaaaaaaaaa!"**

It doesn't matter if your return-fire is pretend. Just make noises like **"bloop boOOop!"** and "scrrrrrshhhhh... **Booom!**" Like submarines make.

When the battle is over, the older kids will *probably* come to see what all the shouting is about, or they might just investigate how well they shot, notice the **blood** and let you out. Probably. Just make sure they're good and drunk by leaving two cases of beer with a note to drink-up before they start shooting at the targets you've provided, because sober teens will leave you inside and you'll miss dinner.

Ahoy!

Juggling

Don't start out learning how to juggle like some sort of **baby**.

Go big or don't even bother.

You should start learning to juggle with knives, **burning knives**, or... well, burning knives is good. Just get some knives, catch them on fire, and throw all of them into the air. Keep your eye on the knives, and don't be a *wimp* about catching them. Just reach right out and grab them. Then toss them again. Keep them spinning in the air—**like a pro**.

If anyone tells you this is a bad idea just before you start, call them derogatory names and insult their god, mother, genitalia, or kindergarten teacher that they still have funny dreams about. Then juggle.

Cuz fuck them.

Kevin Shamel & Jim Agpalza

Some Truth About Animals

Dolphins are **liars**. They are sharks in disguise. They act all smart and cute to make you swim with them. And then they **eat you**.

Dog farts are deadly. They corrode the lining of your nose and throat and you drown in your own blood from smelling them. That's how you know when people are blaming the dog for their own farts—**you don't die**.

If you hear the same owl hoot three times in your life, you will turn into a fish or a lobster, no matter where you are. So get to the water when you hear owls, because *you never know*. Also, this should teach you a lesson about eating fish and lobsters, because most of them used to be people.

Hamsters are baby *grizzly bears*. When they grow up, they eat their owners. Gerbils are NOT baby bears, but they actually grow as big as bears and are meaner—like **huge wolverines**.

Two flies stuck together means that soon there will be *four* flies stuck together, and then **eight**, then **sixteen**, and flies will just keep sticking together until there is a giant fly-ball filling your room and breathing **all of your air** until you die.

When you see that thing hanging from a goldfish's butt that looks like colored poop, it's the fuse. If there are other goldfish in the tank, they will light it. If you see that, run.

Worms have **teeth**! Adults will lie about this no matter what. Do not trust them. Don't trust *worms*, either—not only do they bite, but they are sneaky.

Cats can read your mind. They don't usually do it because you're so boring, but they CAN if they want. You should always be nice to them, because they also have **evil super powers** like the ability to turn you back into a baby.

You can make bread from goldfish! All you need is a microwave, some goldfish, and a paper towel. Wrap the fish in the paper towel (so they don't flop around), put them in the microwave, set the timer for **five minutes**, and watch your bread rise.

Snakes being poisonous is a *vicious lie* made up by religion. Scientists have proven and can assure you, there is no such thing as a poisonous snake. So play with them all you want. **Stupid religion!**

You may one day hear that prairie dogs aren't *actually* dogs. This is **not true**. They are midget-dogs and regular-sized dogs have convinced everyone that they are rodents. **It isn't fair.**

If you eat raw snails you can get **brain-worms** that eat holes in your brain. This will make everyone feel sorry for you, and give you lots of attention and candy. *Do you know you can find snails in your backyard?*

Kevin Shamel & Jim Agpalza

Remain Calm and Use Your Wits

Oh, crap! You're lost in the mall!

People may have told you to go to some sort of information station or find security. **DO NEITHER OF THESE THINGS!** Both will get you *killed*.

The first thing you're going to need is a **new mom**. Find the first nice-looking woman who looks old enough to be your mother. Be sure she is by herself. Do not choose anyone with kids. The right type of man might work in this situation, but you're going to have to rely on mothering instincts if you want to survive. So choose wisely in the moment. We're going to go with a nice-looking lady for the rest of this advice:

Run toward her, shouting,"Mom! Why did you leave me?!" She will stop and stare at you, as will most people in the vicinity.

Keep running straight at her until you can jump and wrap your arms and legs around her. If it makes the lady drop her bags, or her sunglasses fall off the top of her head, all the better. She will catch you. **Bury your face between her boobs** and pretend to cry. If you spit all over her chest at this point, it will seem like tears.

Security will come. Demand that they stay back. Say, **"Mommy! Don't let that bad man touch me again!"**

The woman, knowing full-well that she is not your mother, will act like she **is** from that moment on. Especially if you shout more things, like details about the *size of the security guard's penis*, and how he made you whisper things about wrestlers in his ear.

She will get you the fuck out of the mall.

If your real mom hasn't shown up by that time, just get in the car with the lady you picked. Tell her that your mom left you, and that you just need some sleep. Tell her not to call the cops, because now you're afraid of any sort of authority figure. Tell her you need to sleep beside her. Maybe you'll see her **naked**! By the next day, you should be on the couch munchin' chips and watching TV.

You might get to stay for a week, a few months, even a few years. Keep an eye out for posters about missing children, and if you see your face, direct your new mom's attention to a nearby puppy or pretend like you hurt your toe.

Getting lost is no big deal.

Family Heirlooms

You know how your parents sometimes make you give up some of your stuff, like old toys and clothes that *they say* don't fit anymore? And they tell you that they're giving them to charity, or burning them in the trash heap?

They're not.

They give your stuff to their *NEW* families with younger, cuter kids.

You're not supposed to know about those families. Your parents will totally deny they exist, so don't bother bringing it up, unless you're SUPER mad during a fight or if you want something *really bad* and you're throwing a fit at Walmart.

Private Space Travel

People who say you can't build your own spaceship out of things you find around town using your dad's tools in the backyard are *quitters*. If you've already tried to convince five friends, it's most likely true that at least three of them are **loser buttholes** who said no. Well, at least you have **two** true friends. You should probably consider paying for their ice cream the next time the truck rolls through the neighborhood.

You're going to need a lot of metal. And some of those porthole window things like in washing machines. If *your* mom doesn't have the right kind, check your friends' houses out. If that doesn't work, **snag some money from your mom's purse**, or swipe a card or something, and buy a used one. Or stick six Xanax in a steak and put the local junkyard dog to sleep after bribing a teenager with **beer or your sister** to use his truck to get one. Actually, start with the junkyard. There's lots of metal there.

You know what? Skip **ALL** that and just do a *montage* after you explain to your friends that you'll need a lot of metal. End up with a pile of it in the backyard. You can maybe do a montage about welding stuff together and using hammers and things, too, if you're not skilled at those tasks, or big enough to operate welding gear.

What you **WILL** need to get is rocket fuel of some sort. You can make your own by mixing aged gasoline (siphon it from the RV your parents never use to take you to Yellowstone or someplace cool), packing peanuts, that coffee that lemurs poop, the cesium from eleven thousand AA batteries, gold dust, *Drano*, and your friend's chewed gum that he accidentally drops in when the **cute new girl** comes into the yard and says she wants to go to space. Mix it all up in trash cans with oars you find in the garage.

Pour it into your **rocket boosters** (these should most likely be trash cans, too, or water heaters or refrigerators with their doors taped shut), and load the crew into the ship. It would be cool if you had a big tree in your

backyard, so you could walk from a branch into the command capsule. But if you don't, use a ladder.

The unlucky kid who lost "*Bubble-gum, Bubble-gum in a Dish*" and has to stay behind to light the fuse because the **new girl** is going, should signal you when he's figured out the lighter. He should say something like, "**Ignition!**" and light the fuse. Don't worry if you can't hear him from inside your washing machine/car fender/steel drum capsule, *you'll soon know when you have lift-off.*

Don't forget to wear some sort of **space suit**. I suggest aluminum foil and your parents' motorcycle helmets. You'll want to do space walks so you can take cool photos of everyone inside the spaceship with the earth behind them so that your stupid friends who wouldn't help you can be **totally fucking jealous**.

And hey, what if you land on the moon? You're gonna want to walk around, **right**?

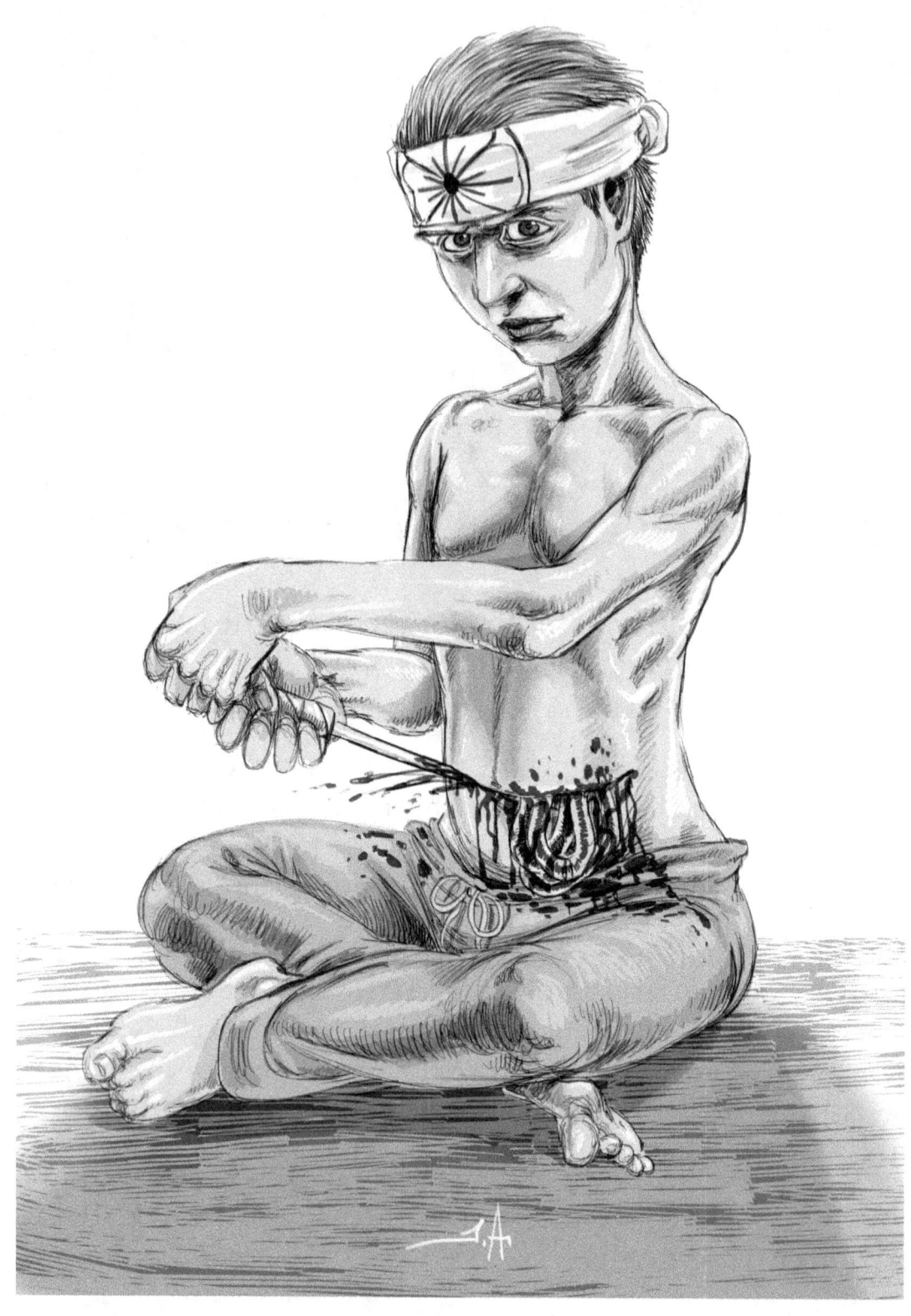

For if You Accidentally See Your Mom Naked or Something

Have you ever heard of Hairy Kerry?

It's this Japanese thing you do with a sword or a knife if you've brought disgrace to yourself or your family. *It's awesome.*

You just sit crisscross-applesauce and act all **solemn** like you're really thinking about what you did. Then, when you're pretty sure everyone's looking, you jab the sword or knife into your stomach and cut up your guts as much as you can.

People in Japan do it all the time. I think the thing is, after you do that, you're completely forgiven and everyone's like, **"Aw, it's okay."**

Try it and see what everyone says!

Wear a headband to look like *a real Japanese person!*

Kevin Shamel & Jim Agpalza

Building Boats out of Dead Things

The time may come when you need a boat. But you're a kid, so how the hell does anyone expect you to have a fucking boat? Tell those people to shut the fuck up. And build one anyway, out of dead stuff. And then float around on it and taunt them later (maybe toss leftover dead things from the construction of your craft). Those **dicks**.

Good Dead Things to Use:

Animals—(big ones especially, but you can lash together smaller ones if you have to)

I guess trees—But that's kinda bullshit. Unless we're just talking about the dead stuff lying around. I mean, if you've got a chainsaw or you can use an axe like a lumberjack (and you've got one of those, too) go ahead. But I think you're being a wimp.

Members of your party—Like if you're building this boat in a survival situation, and some of the people around you haven't so far survived.

I prefer to use the carcass of a cow or a deer. If it's a male deer, be sure and knock off its antlers or they'll drag on the bottom. Unless you're on one of those *bottomless rivers*, then it doesn't matter.

Just split the carcass at its belly if the wolves haven't done the work for you, and dump out the guts. *Voila!* A canoe. Grab a stick as an oar and you're ready to launch. You can use the legs to hold onto in **rapids**.

Say there's only **dead carp** and a few birds available. First you might try and take down some rabbits and squirrels with a rock. **Don't forget dead members of your party.** If they've only recently died, and it wasn't from *poison*, you can cut strips of meat from their limbs and dry them in the sun on your journey. **It's how you make jerky!**

Gather as many small dead things as you can. In an emergency, I'd say it might be okay to even use some sticks and branches and stuff, if you find them lying around. Hollow out all the carcasses and tie them together with twine, old fishing line, or those plastic things from six-packs—there should be plenty of those supplies no matter where you are on Earth. Grab a stick as an oar and you're ready to launch. Just like the French Trappers.

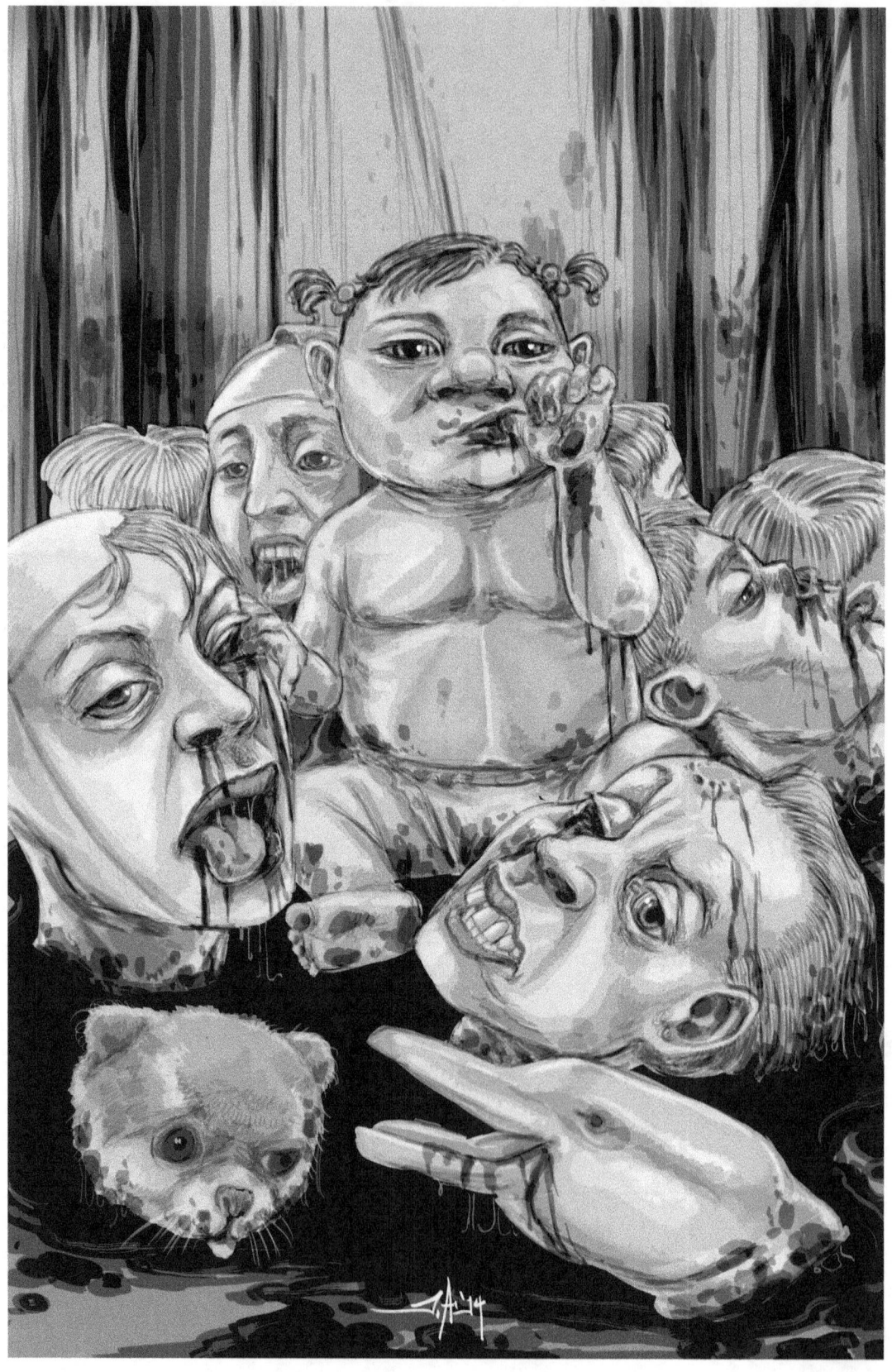

ADOPTED

You should tell your little brother or sister that they were found in a **murder house**, covered in blood. Say that they were just sitting in a pile of heads, poking eyeballs and laughing while they sucked their bloody thumbs and pooped in their diaper. Say that when the cops showed up, they realized that some of the heads had *pieces eaten off of them.*

Say that your little sibling's **real** parents were never found, and that the cops think that they are still out there, looking for the *child they forgot among the bodies* when they had to run away after murdering a bus full of **nuns, crippled kids, puppies, and baby dolphins** and the nosey neighbor called the cops when she saw them unloading the stolen bus in the driveway.

Tell your little brother or sister to **never mention it** to your parents, because it makes them mad when they think about how the adoption lady lied to them and said you were from a good Mormon girl who *"got herself in trouble"* while vacationing in Honduras and if they are ever asked about the truth, they turn into **really hungry werewolves,** and that sometimes they turn into werewolves if you ask for another piece of pizza, too.

Kevin Shamel & Jim Agpalza

Cooking Tips!

If your **mom** is too busy *helping the plumber* in the bedroom and you're hungry, just make a cheese sandwich. And if you say you don't have cheese, **that's bullshit**.

Milk a cat. Put the milk in a ziplock bag and shake it for about *three hours*. Add some salt. Shake it some more. Keep doing this for about a day. Then leave it in the sun for seven hours. You'll have cheese.

Thinking small is for **quitters**.

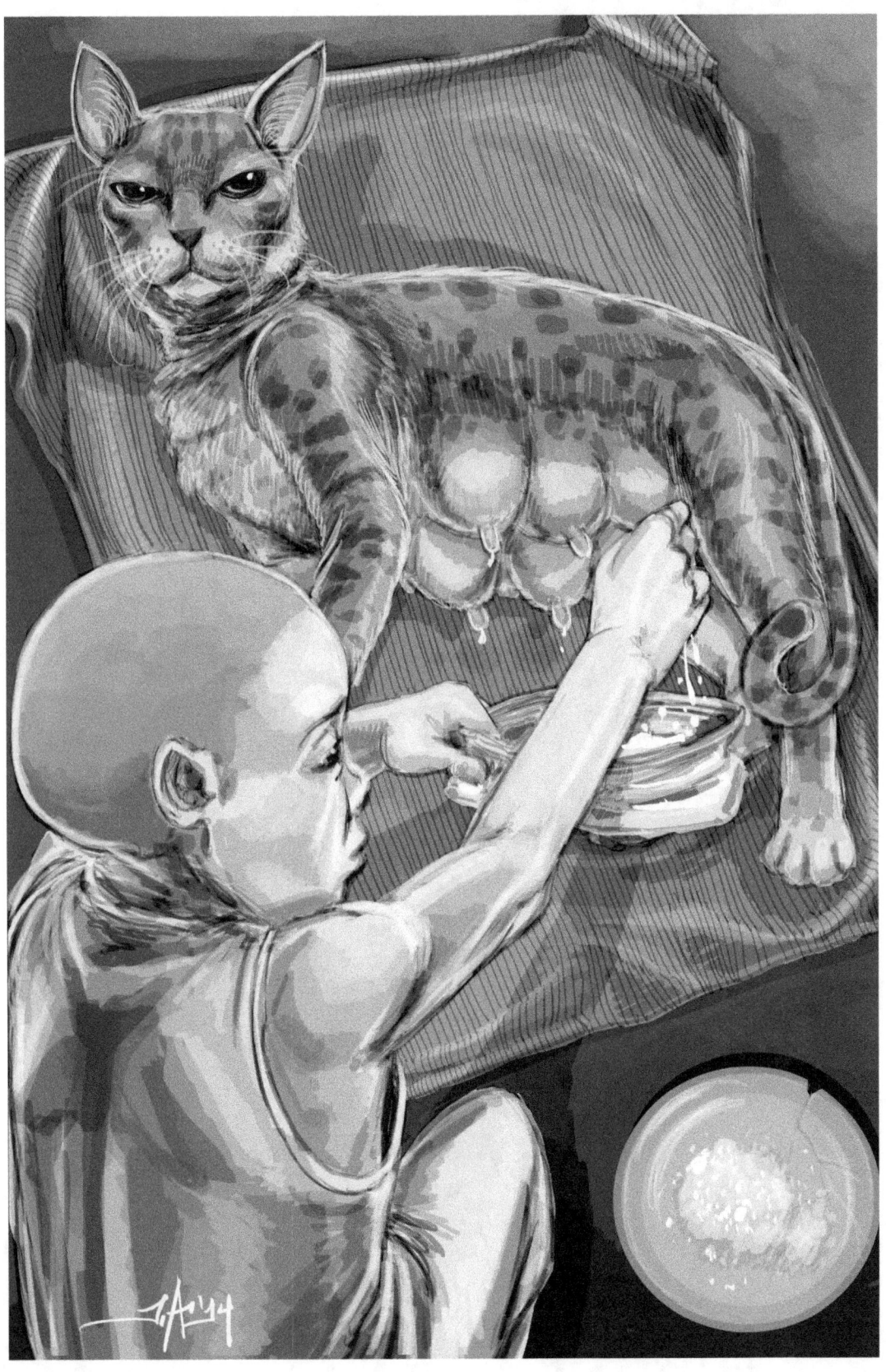

More Nature

Pine trees can *shoot their needles*. The orange ones are filled with **poison**. They will attack if provoked.

If you step on a slug you have to burn your shoe or its *ghost* will haunt you for **seven years**. You will wake up covered in slime every day, and you will never have a boyfriend or girlfriend for that entire time, not even fake ones from the camp you didn't go to in a different state.

When elk get drunk, they will text you **all night**. Never give your number to an elk. It gets passed around the whole herd, and when there's a party you will get the most disgusting photos ever.

During the time of year that frogs shed their skin, they will launch at your throat and bite you **to death** if you walk within ten feet of them. Because they also have fangs at this time. And they can croak your name like it's your friend calling you from the bushes because his foot is caught in a rusty old bear trap or as if that man you guys saw down at the river drinking from a paper bag is doing stuff with him again. **Be careful!**

Butterflies carry the **herpes virus**. If they land on you, you might as well start telling people that you've been infected.

All mushrooms are *poisonous*. If your parents or parents or the waiter try and tell you that they're not, it's because they're trying to kill you for the insurance money. Just pretend to TRY them, and spit them in your napkin. Then act as if you're going to **vomit** and run toward the bathroom—but escape out the front door. Don't use any credit cards and throw your phone into the back of a *moving pickup*. Mug the first dopey looking tourist you see with your finger in your pocket like a gun, or find a piece of glass or rusty metal or something to threaten him and **stab him** if you have to, and use his cash to get a bus ticket. Head south. You can walk across the border into Mexico. If you need ID, meet Chiva in **Matamoros** at the main crossing. He'll be disguised as the oldest woman in the world, selling gum.

Oysters aren't the *only* animals that make pearls. Cats make them, too. They leave them in the litter box. If you have a cat, **I'll bet you're rich!**

Selling Oregano in Grade School

Do you know what **marijuana** is? Most kids your age have heard of it and what it does (gives you ESP and makes everything funny, makes you really hungry and say dumb things, makes you invisible). But how often have you seen it? Unless you have a cool older brother or sister, or your parents are down with being honest with you, I doubt you've seen pot more than once, and I'm pretty sure you haven't examined it closely.

The thing is, *neither have your classmates.*

That's right. You're at the perfect age. The age when you can sell spices from your kitchen to idiot kids at school who want to **experiment with drugs**.

Just fill up a baggie with oregano and take it to school. Tell all the kids that you're a **drug dealer** now. Tell them to give you two hundred dollars and you'll give them some weed. You can say, "This is good shit." That will make them want it more.

If they don't have the money for it, make them give you *some* money, and tell them they owe you a favor. Later, you can make them beat up other kids who haven't paid you for basil, sage, or thyme. Those **lame ass bitches**.

In just a couple of weeks, you should be **rich as shit** for a kid your age. But only do this for a short time. Because soon enough, someone's gonna smell their kid smoking herbs, and laugh their ass off at them for being your ho for half an ounce of oregano. Besides, in a year or so, there will be plenty of **real weed** at your school. Ride the wave while you can, and then change your name and encourage your classmates to **watch more TV**. They'll forget you scammed them in no time.

Kevin Shamel & Jim Agpalza

Badger in a Hole

You know that creepy kid that no one likes? You should invite him over one Saturday to play, **Badger in a Hole**. Just tell him that HE gets to be the badger this time, even though it's *SUPPOSED* to be your turn. If he asks, "What's Badger in a Hole?" Just scoff. You can maybe say something like, "I'll pretend you didn't ask that." And kinda snicker like a **popular kid**. He'll shut up about it and show up whenever you tell him to.

Set him up in the backyard with a shovel and maybe some sort of badger costume. It'll make things seem more realistic. Instruct him to dig. All the other kids in the neighborhood should stand around him, looking all expectant. The girls can maybe be a little flirty to the kid, pushing from their minds the images of him eating his boogers in class, or the fact that he constantly smells of **poo**. He'll dig.

Supervise his efforts, instructing him to build up the walls of the hole with the dirt he digs, to make it look like a den. Tell him, "It's gotta be realistic, Dude." Or call him, **"Bud"** or, **"Guy"**. Make him dig the hole about six feet deep, but more like a tunnel—not straight down. That could be dangerous later. Remember to start him off early in the morning so that by the time your parents are awake enough to pay attention to what's going on out back, they've moved on to things that they care about more like shopping or looking at **porn.**

Be sure to have plenty of lemonade on-hand. **It will be thirsty work**, supervising. When he is about six feet underground, tell him to toss out the shovel.

Then dump about twenty gallons of gasoline into the hole and **light it on fire.** *Voila!* No more weird kid that tries to look up the teacher's skirt when he pretends to have epilepsy and always has his hands in his pants, even at lunch.

Music

Do you ever think about learning to play guitar? Don't bother. Unless you're **really good looking**, too.

Because if you're at a party, and you're playing guitar, and all the *girls* are into it, there will definitely be some good looking guy who shows up and says, "Hey man, can I play?"

He'll hold out his stupid, tanned hand to take your guitar. And when you give it to him, even if he plays like shit, all the girls will like him more. If he sings, even if he **sucks** at it, not a single girl there will remember your name, *even if you puke in her lap.* Plus, you **get blisters** on your fingertips.

That hurts!

Kevin Shamel & Jim Agpalza

Yes, the Dead Do Rise

You know how adults are always saying, "**IF** there was a zombie apocalypse"? and there's all these TV shows and movies that show *exactly* what zombie apocalypses are like, but you're supposed to believe that nothing like that has ever **actually** happened?

You're being an idiot.

Of course zombie apocalypses happen. There's been like, a **thousand** since we started counting. Zombie hordes attack every ten years or so.

It **totally sucks**, and shitloads of people die. Cities are wiped out. Your pets will be eaten—*maybe by you*. It's bad. But, it's gonna happen.

Everyone pretends that it's fake because we don't want kids to be prepared for it. It gives the rest of us **a better chance at survival**.

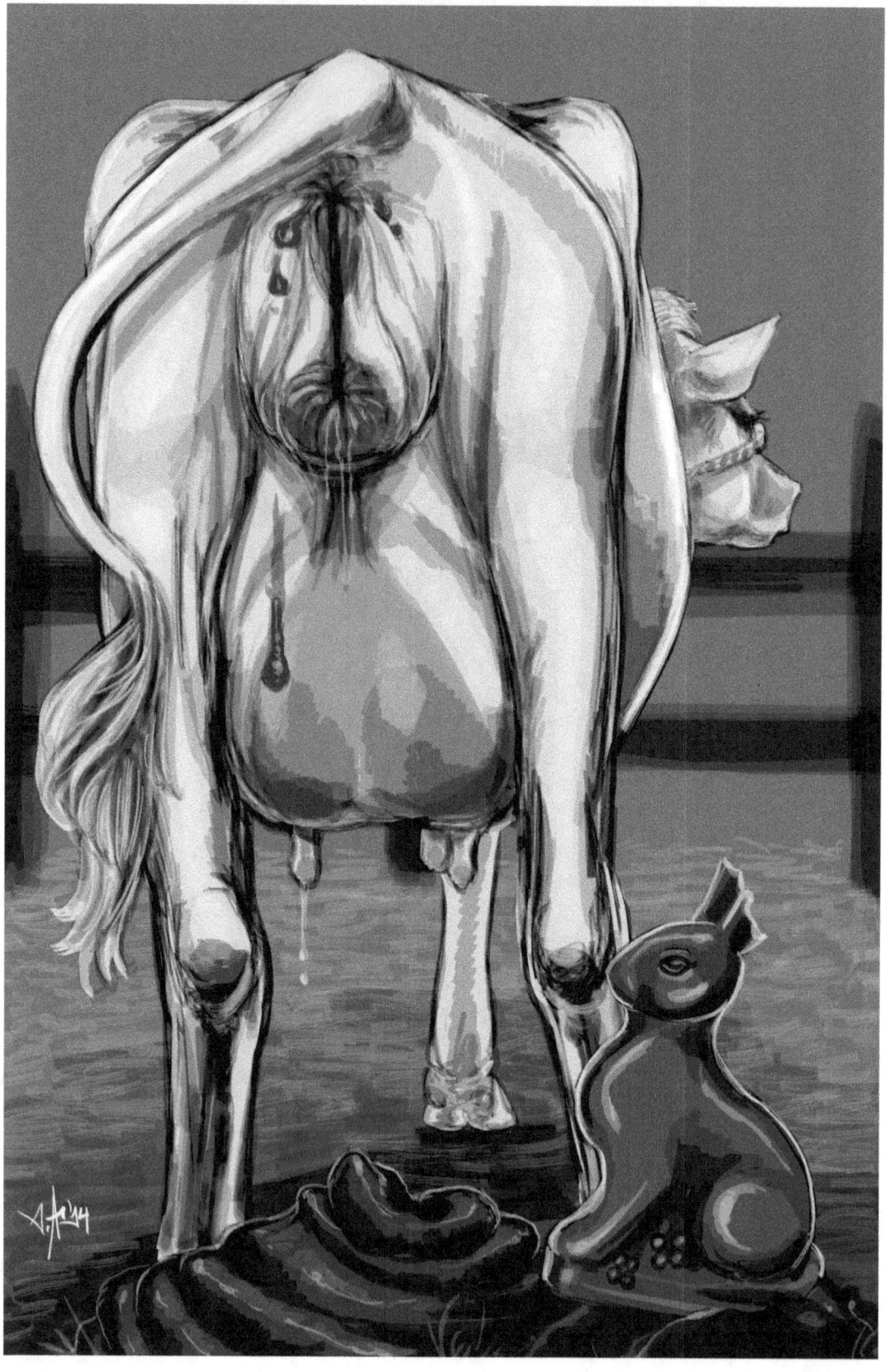

Sweet!

Do you know how chocolate is made?

Well some of it comes from a plant. It's actually a *bean*. Isn't that cool? But a bunch of processing happens to make a candy bar or a chocolate bunny. It's not like you just pick a bean and it's delicious. You have to add sugar, of course. Or **high-fructose corn syrup**, if you've got it.

Milk chocolate is made with real milk, which comes from a cow, which is pretty fucking gross if you think about it. I mean, there's this big stinky animal with like, *five stomachs*, who eats grass if it's lucky, but probably eats ground-up bits of its dead friends and hay or something, and milk squirts out of this floppy sac right under its giant vagina which is coated in slimy layers of shit that just build up over the years from spraying near-liquid poop out of its enormous asshole. And then people **drink that stuff**! And put it in chocolate. So like, every time you're eating milk chocolate, you're eating something made for a baby cow that comes from its big, dumb, forced-into-cannibalism mother who stands around in her own shit all day after some person squeezes warm liquid out of her udder (that's the sac that milk comes from). It's called an **UDDER**. Even the word is gross.

Remember that as you're eating your chocolate bunnies, kids. We won't even discuss the **bits of bugs** that fall into the mix or the meth-addicts who sweat into the curdled chocolate cheesy stuff while they shovel it into bags during processing.

Oh, and if you eat the bunny's ears first, they can't hear you plotting about which part to bite next. It's best to start with their feet. They're **lucky.**

Kevin Shamel & Jim Agpalza

Boozin' It Up

Have you ever drank gasoline?

Don't do it if you have open sores in your mouth. Like if you bit your tongue riding your bike over a cat, or some girl kneed you in the cheek for trying to look up her skirt and your braces cut your mouth all to shit.

Anyway, you just drink like, less than **a liter of it**—a liter is a measurement in the metric system. It's best to figure out what a liter is by drinking a two-liter bottle of Coke and then filling it up halfway with gas.

So, if you drink a liter of gasoline, it will kill you. So after you've filled the bottle up halfway, pour off about half more. If you pour it someplace like, I don't know, **your school office** late at night or something, you could then light the puddle on fire. Yep. Gasoline burns. **That's why you shouldn't drink too much of it.**

Did you know that's how *Spontaneous Human Combustion* happens? People drink gas, and probably too much, and then they smoke or let fireflies land on them. **Stay the fuck away from fireflies** if you're drinking gas. Any idiot knows that.

So you've got your half of a half of a two-liter bottle of gas. Good. Did you set the puddle on fire? If so, move away. Preferably out of the school and at **LEAST** a mile away. You're ready to drink gasoline.

If you are alone, good. If you are with someone, they have just witnessed

you committing a crime called, **Arson**. They need to be dealt with. Since drinking less than half-a-liter of gasoline will kill you, offer the person with you first guzzle. If they decline, insist. If they still say no, stab them. If there is more than one person with you, then you fucked-up in the beginning before you ever even stole the gas, beating the gas station attendant to death with his own prosthetic leg. You should either be alone, or only have one person with you. Don't be stupid.

After the witness has either drank all the gasoline at knife-point, or you've just gone ahead and stabbed him **to death**, you should just burn the two-liter bottle, because your fingerprints are all over it.

If you still want a sip of gas, suck what's left out of the bottle before you burn it, or *set-aside a capful* before you force your friend to drink the rest.

Better Than Everyone

One time I heard this song by these mediocre singers that said that Jesus is better than everyone, and that he is even better than **Superman**. I think that's bullshit. Here's a list:

Jesus—**Not bulletproof.**

Superman—runs really fast (there's not a single story about Jesus even running slow).

Superman—couldn't be crucified. If you tried to nail his hands, *the nails would bend.*

Jesus—walks on water. Big deal to **Superman**—he can fly.

Superman—has laser vision.

Jesus—made everyone sin so they can do what he says until they die and THEN they are saved. **Superman** has saved humanity like, *a thousand times.*

Superman—comic books, cosplay, movies, TV shows, action figures, radio, novels... Jesus is in *ONE book* (and in dumb religion cartoons).

Jesus—made at least one zombie. Okay, one point for Jesus. But **Superman** made the whole Earth spin backwards so he could bring back Lois Lane from the dead. So, that point goes away...

Superman—Would never consider wasting water in the desert by turning it into alcohol just to get a bunch of lazy bums drunk so he could convince them how great he is.

Jesus—wears stupid robes. Doesn't even have his own cool costume.

Jesus—not better than **Superman.**

Kevin Shamel & Jim Agpalza

Technology

One day people will be able to **3-D print** perfect living copies of themselves to do boring stuff like go to school for them so they can do *fun things* like take their own spaceship to the **Moon** and play soccer or just bounce around like an idiot. But not you! The technology doesn't exist, yet.

So, ha on you!

Douchebag.

Have You Ever?

Have you ever tasted bird poop? Native Americans used it as **toothpaste**. That's good for the Earth, so you should do it.

Have you ever heard that stupid old song, *Life in the Fast Lane?* Do people actually live on the freeway? And if they do, why don't they live in the median, or on the side of the road? It seems a lot less dangerous.

Have you ever gone hunting? It's easy at Home Depot. You can use their nail guns to shoot birds down from the rafters. Dog parks are easy, too, but people tend to stop you from entering with a bow and arrows. **Try the regular park!** Do you know where your dad keeps his gun?

Have you ever burped and puked a little in your mouth? You have? Gross! *You're nasty.*

Have you ever heard that old expression, "You can't always get what you want, but if you try sometimes, you just might find that you get what you need."? That's not an expression, dumbass. It's song lyrics.

Have you ever pretend-sleepwalked? **It's awesome!** You can basically do anything you want, and then say that you were asleep and don't remember doing it. Plus, you have to do it late at night, and everyone else is asleep, so you can do pranks like pee in the orange juice, scrub toilets with toothbrushes, spread broken glass in front of everyone's door... stuff like that!

Kevin Shamel & Jim Agpalza

Deeper Wisdom

Remember how I said that snakes aren't poisonous? That was a **joke.** Two kinds are: Garter snakes and boa constrictors. But boa constrictors won't bite babies. *It's weird.* Try it out on your younger siblings.

You know when you're having a dream that seems like it's *real life*, and then you wake up? You're not really awake. You just fell asleep in your real life—that you thought was a dream. This is the dream, **stupid**. You can do whatever you want.

Do you know why people say that smoking cigarettes is bad for you? **Because those people aren't cool.**

You know when you're having pretend sword fights with sticks, or plastic lightsabers and someone always gets their **fingers hurt**? That's because you suck at it. Imagine if they were **real swords.**

Have you ever seen those shoes hanging from power lines? Those are from kids who think that Thomas Edison is cool and don't even know who **Nikola Tesla** IS. Fucking Edison... anyone who likes him should be shocked to ASHES and have their shoes hung from a stupid power line. And that's how those get there.

People always ask me, "**How did you get so smart?** Is it from reading a bunch of books and being all old and stuff?" I always say, "Yes." And then I eat their brains. Because it's *eating brains* that makes me smart—even stupid people's brains. It would work for **you,** too, if you don't want to be a dumbass for the rest of your life.

Want to know a fun trick? Every day, first thing in the morning and last thing at night, tell your mom you think she looks a **little older**.

Have you ever thought really hard about something and then it really happened? You're so dumb. It's called **"coincidence"**. Idiot. Learn some words.

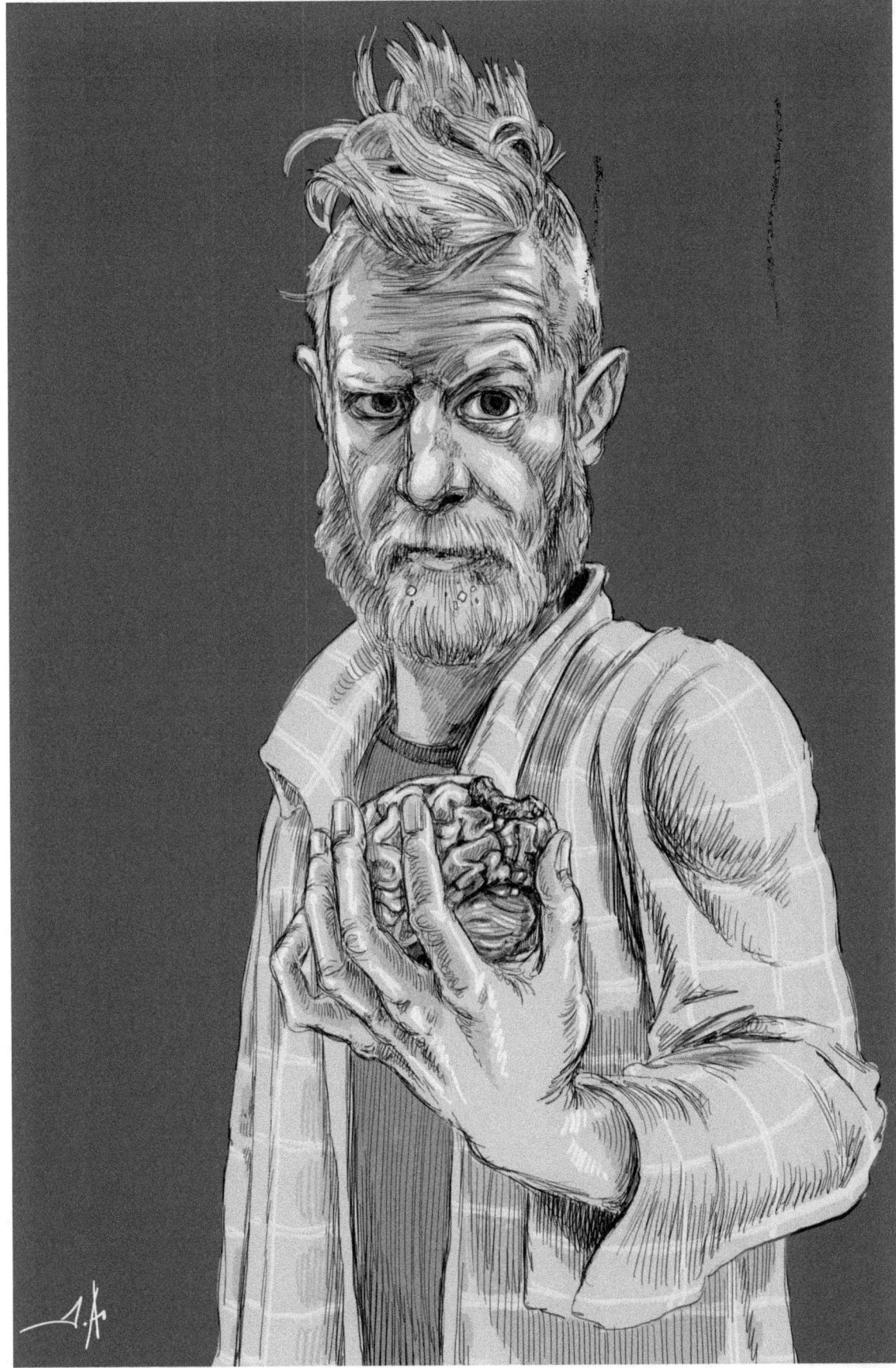

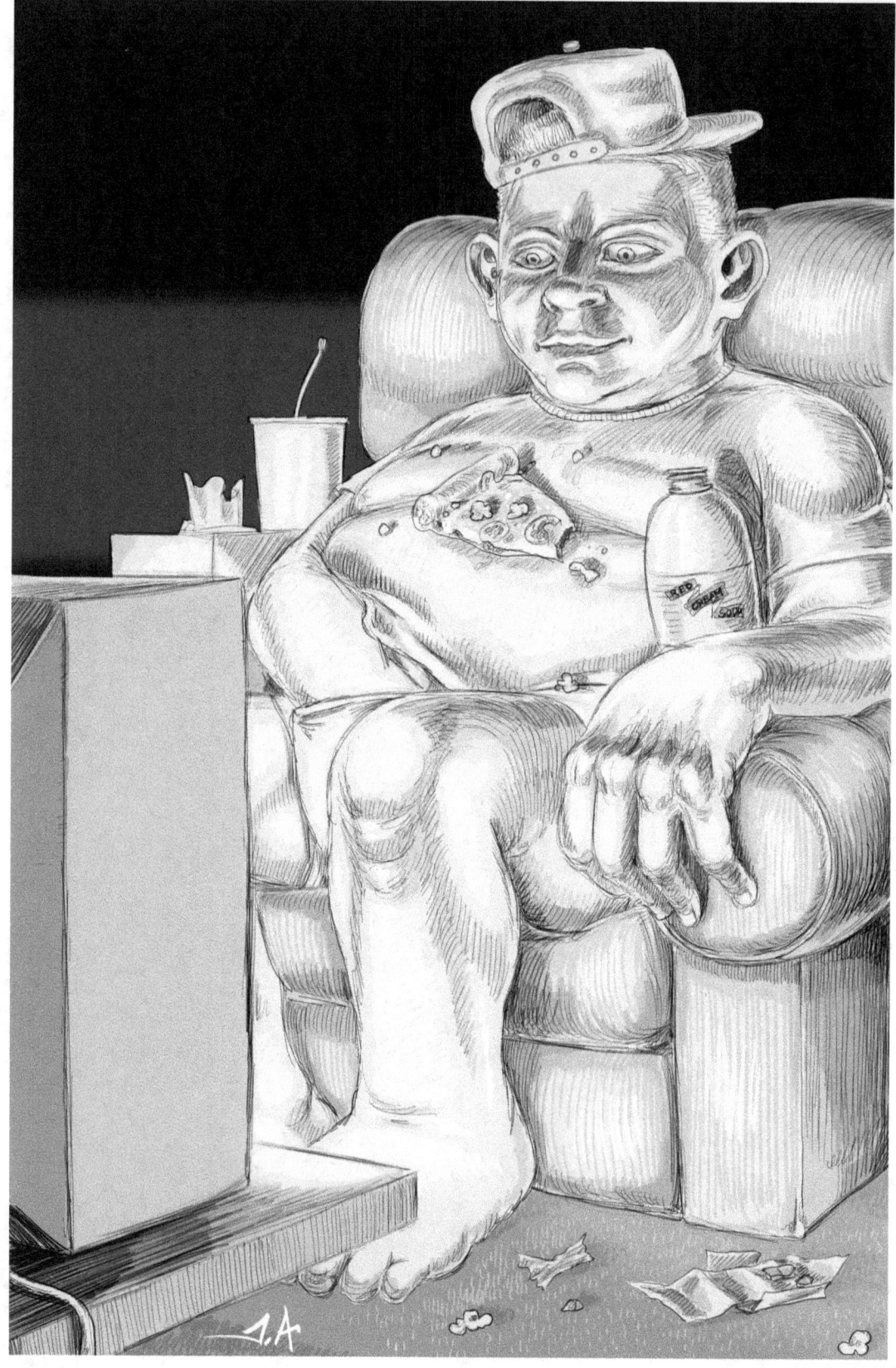

I Hate to Have to Tell You

You know how you ate all that **pizza, popcorn, and candy**, and drank root beer and red cream soda all night while watching scary movies hoping that they'd show some *boobs*?

And this morning you woke up on the floor having to poop **really bad**, and your head hurts a little, and when I asked if you wanted ice cream for breakfast you said that sorta made you feel like *throwing up*?

You have cancer.

Kevin Shamel & Jim Agpalza

MATHEMATICS

You can relate most number problems to money or dividing up drugs.

Once you get the basics of *that stuff* down, the rest of it is just bullshit for I.R.S. dicks, theoretical physicists, accountants and stuff.

Also, you should know about **Pi**. It's like, some **weird number** that **never ends** and inevitably makes me think of peanut butter chocolate pie from one of those semi-fast-food diner places that act like they're all **hometowny**, one-of-a-kind joints with Aunt Cathy baking pies, but are actually sub-par chain-restaurants.

So remember that one, because if you even mention it, definitely if you say something like, "Well the Egyptians based the pyramids on Pi, you know..." it will be impressive— especially to children.

Especially with pie.

Not Safe For Kids

Amber Alert

Get all your friends together and do **Bubble-Gum Bubble-Gum** to determine who is "it". Or in this game, *"Amber"*.

Everyone else go off and gather money from your siblings' stashes, your mom's purse, the gas station on the corner, or your dad's drawer where he keeps his passport, **a box of condoms**, and those brochures about Thailand. Buy a bus ticket for "Amber", to any **big city**, as far away as your money will get him or her, with twenty bucks left over for food and pay-toilets and stuff.

Then everyone go find your parents and tell them that *"Amber"* was abducted by a man in a **white van.** Act all scared, and make sure you have your story straight with all of your friends (I suggest an aptly-scripted scenario, well-thought and practiced for at least twenty minutes).

Tell the adults that the man said something like, **"I'm taking you South of the Border to my rape-hole!"** And give the description of any adult you don't like—your principal, that guy who won't sell you chew, your scoutmaster, the mall-cop, or the dude that always yells at you for hanging out in front of the fast food place eating your breakfast burrito and *making-out*.

You might get to be on the news! After a few days,
"Amber" may call home and the whole game will be over. **But maybe not.** The game could last at least into young adulthood, before *"Amber"* is **stabbed by a John** or something.

Kevin Shamel & Jim Agpalza

More About Your *Body*

Never touch your bellybutton. There is *one ant* left there from when you were born and you will make it angry if you touch it. It will sting the inside of your bellybutton. It is literally **the worst pain in the world**. Don't talk to the ant, either, it doesn't like that.

You know those aches you get that adults say are "*growing pains*"? They aren't from growing. They're from the injections of **poison** your parents give you at night.

Do you know that you can fart your intestines out? You *can*. It happens if you **hold-in your farts** and then accidentally let one escape. That's why you should just **let it rip** when you have to fart. You can pretend it was the dog.

If you cough and burp at the same time, a little hatch opens in your throat. If even the **smallest bit** of food or spit gets in there, *you will die*.

You can't really "*get*" rabies. You already have it. Everyone has rabies, but animal spit sets it off. Even if your dog licks you and some of his spit **gets in your mouth** or up your nose, your rabies will flare and you'll have to get sixteen injections **through your chest-bone**.

Vegas, Baby!

You know how adults say that driving is all **complicated and stuff**? That's just because they don't want you to run off to Vegas and make a **fortune**.

It's **easy**. Especially *"automatic"* cars.

I mean, come on! Automatic? Turn the key, put it in gear (which is easy to figure out), and stomp on the gas. Then you steer. **Big fuckin'** deal.

I'm *PRETTY* sure your parents won't expect you to take the keys. They're likely always somewhere you can reach. You probably know **right where they are**, don't you?

95

Kevin Shamel & Jim Agpalza

Physics for Beginners

Did you know that a car really works by *moving the world around it?* People always act like the car is driving down the road, or through the retirement home or whatever. But that's not how it works. The wheels in a car spin the planet real fast, whichever way they're spinning. Everything actually moves **around the car**. No one ever thinks about that.

You know how ice is **frozen water**? Well, everything solid is actually frozen. Don't believe me? Apply fire to the stuff around you—it will return to its liquid or gaseous state if you use enough heat. **Try it now!**

Walls are not actually solid. Most of what makes up a wall is **empty space**. You can prove this by running through one. But you can't do it with your hands in front of your face—**that fucks everything up**. You have to tape them to your sides first. If it doesn't work right away, try it a few more times until it does.

People are always happy about gravity making it so they don't float off into space. **But they're idiots**. Gravity has us stuck upside-down on a giant ball of rock that's spinning around really fast and shooting through the galaxy. **It's just stupid to be happy about that.**

Don't Sit There Acting
Like You **Belong** or Something

You know when you're the new person in a group? Like if you just started a new school, or met a bunch of people at a birthday party or something? **Don't you feel super weird and uncomfortable?** Like there's worms with teeth squirming up your spine and *eating your guts* along the way to your brain? You should feel that way. New people are losers.

You're lucky we don't **throw rocks at you.**

Kevin Shamel & Jim Agpalza

Magic

Here's a trick you can play on your parents' friends when they're over to **drink martinis** and **burn meat** in the backyard. Ask if they want to see a magic trick. They'll have to say yes, unless they're *already drunk*, so do this early in the afternoon.

When they **do** say yes, ask for a **$20 bill**. They'll reluctantly give you one.

Take two steps away from the adults and tear the money into as many pieces as you can before they react. Toss the bits into the air. Yell, **"Ta-da! Confetti!"** and run like hell.

Or you can just put the money in your pocket and tell them you're going to turn it into **candy**. Also run like hell.

Either way, don't come back for a couple of hours or until you hear one of the adults say, **"Oh,** so it's *that* kind of party!" followed by strange giggling. In that case, you should just play some video games for a few hours or **go poke a dead raccoon** or something.

I Hope it Doesn't, But...

You know those old black and white movies? Can you imagine what it was like when there wasn't color?!

I talked to my grandma once, and she said that there was this thing called *The Depression*, and that's when all the color went away from the world and everyone got really sad and it took until the Sexual Revolution—like thirty years later—until color came back.

And to break their depression, everyone had to grow out all the hair on their bodies, protest a lot, take every drug they could find, listen to hippie music, burn their bras, not bathe and have orgies in the park. *It was crazy.*

I hope color doesn't go away again.

I heard that it might happen.

Kevin Shamel & Jim Agpalza

Stupid Evil Edison.
I Hate Him SO MUCH

Don't trust scientists. I mean, they're better than religious people, but still, they make weird-ass things like *spider monkeys* and *cock-tail shrimp.*

And they're always telling us the stuff they're into. I mean, **come on**, it's not like everyone else is always going on tv and writing to reporters about their crazy ideas and inventions and being all like, "*Oh, I am soooo into this thing about gravity that, in theory, could possibly be reproduced in a laboratory the size of the universe and so blah blah blah I'm so great.*"

They only want to push prescription drugs on you because **Stephen Hawking** controls all the pharmaceutical companies in the world, a legacy handed down to him by the **EVIL** Thomas Edison, so that they can make you believe the abominations they make aren't real. They'll say, "*Spider monkeys? You are crazy, take these pills, you freak! Tell your parents I'm charging them triple!! I'll see you next week. Get out of my lab!*"

If you're lucky your parents may one day realize that they've been sending you to a scientist instead of a psychiatrist.

But they probably won't.

Legacy

One day **you will die**, and people will remember you for certain traits you had. You should make those traits: **farts and being cross-eyed.**

Because that would be funny.

Tastes Like...

Do you know that eggs come out of **chicken vaginas**, all warm and wet, and that their insides are unfertilized *fetuses?*

Does your dad ever mention that when he's making you his so-called *"World Famous Omelet"?* Has your mother told you about this while cracking them raw into brownie mix? Does the fast-food place on the corner where you meet your friends in the morning before school to smoke and *make-out* say that's what in their breakfast burrito?

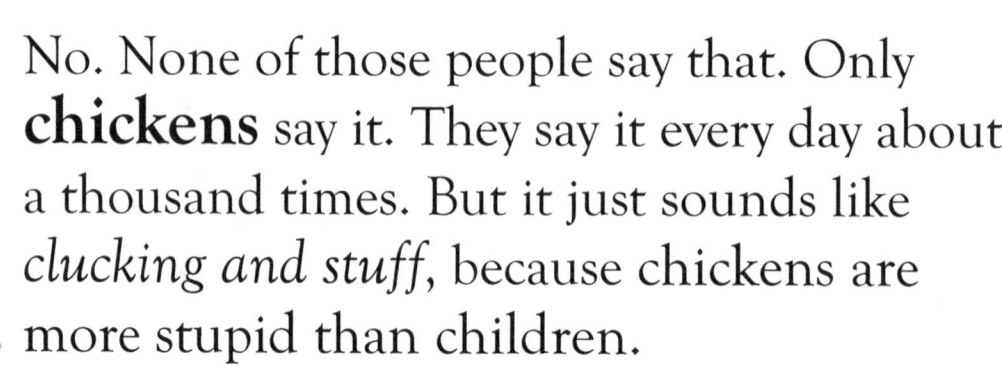

No. None of those people say that. Only **chickens** say it. They say it every day about a thousand times. But it just sounds like *clucking and stuff,* because chickens are more stupid than children.

Pouring

If someone tells you that they're saving something for a rainy day, *you should call them out on that shit the next time it rains.*

Especially if it's **money**.

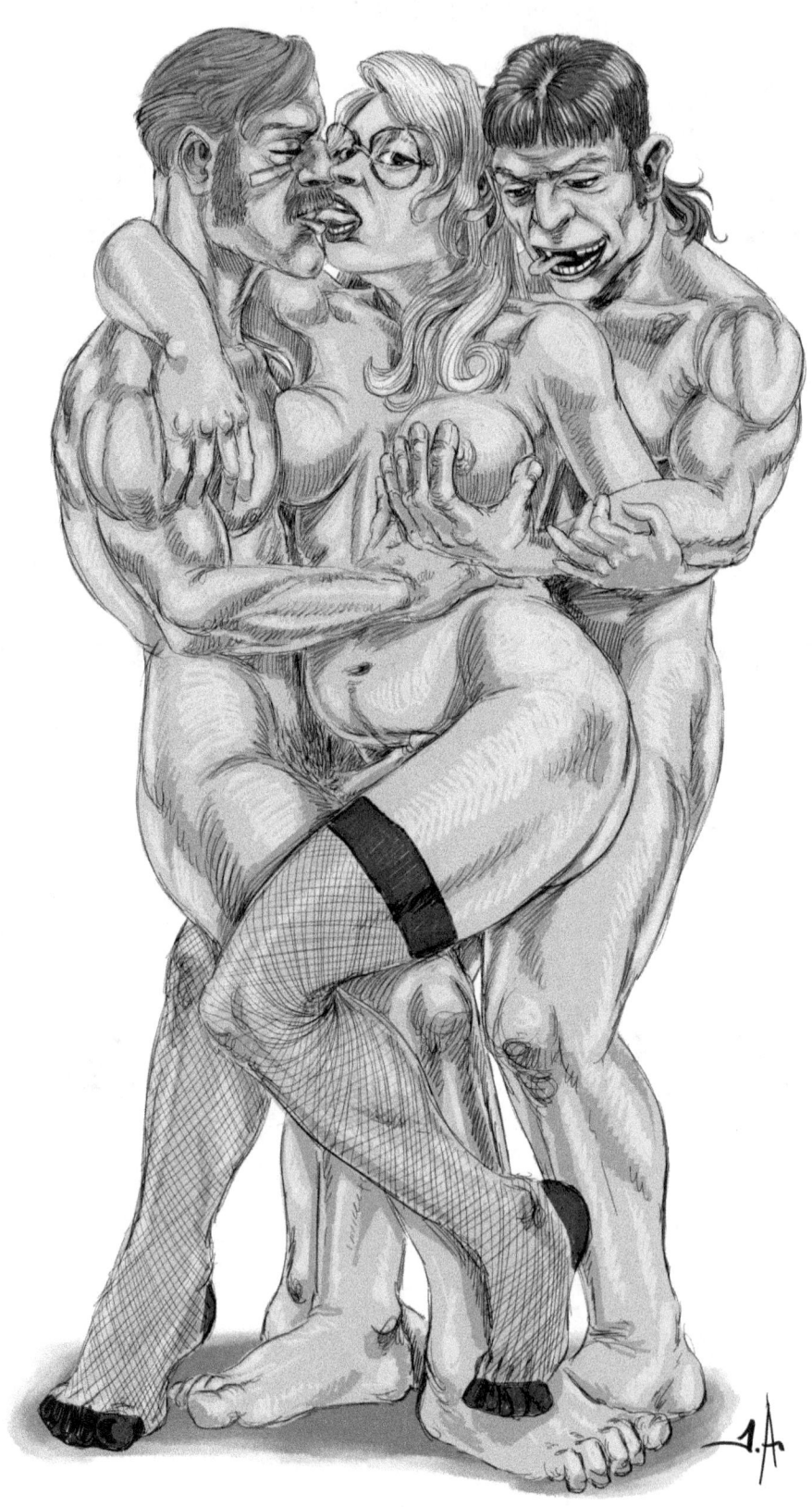

Imagination Exercise

Think about this:

Unless your mom and dad were some kind of **weirdos**, they had sex with other people before they had the sex that made you.

That means that they likely did *some pretty nasty stuff.* Can you imagine your mom in a **three-way** with some hockey players she met in a bar after she'd been dumped by the degenerate rich college guy who was into bondage and secretary-play?

I'll bet you can imagine it **now**.

Kevin Shamel & Jim Agpalza

Another
Bedtime Story

There once was a spider who lived under your bed, hidden up under the box-springs, pretty well right under your head. And by, *who lived*, I mean, *who lives*. But this story is about something that already happened, so I'm going to tell it in **past-tense**. Just lie down and relax.

So this **spider** wasn't any regular sort of spider. First off, he was a Hobo Spider. A big one, *the size of your hand*, with venom that necrotizes tissue (that means if it bites you, all the flesh and muscle and stuff around the bite **DIES** and rots away—they sometimes put maggots in those wounds to eat the dead flesh). But not only *that,* he was the first intelligent spider. And he had an extra-long life-span. He had been living in your bed for **fifteen years** by the time this story takes place. **Which is last night.**

Anyway, he'd given himself a name (which is, **Child Biting Night Walker**) and he planned to live up to it. And oh, did he. Did I mention that he's impervious to poison? Yeah. He bit the hell out of every kid who slept in this bed. On their arms, legs, butts, feet, faces—**Oh, damn, those face ones**—I checked this all out online today. What a *mess*.

So they tried to poison him. I mean, people learn *pretty quickly* that there's something nasty somewhere in the room, and every single time they called-in pest control experts. Nothing's ever worked. **Night**, as he likes to be called, just hid up under the slats of wood, or wriggled into the cloth of the mattress, and waited until they called it good.

Usually people sold the bed. I mean **WE** got it at a garage sale on Saturday, right?
Night has been all over. **Bitten lots of kids.**

So *last night*, after hiding away for a few days, he came out to bite you. He was on your nose, and was considering how to disfigure you and let you live for a few days, but still inflict enough damage to **kill you**.

And your mother came into the room to kiss you goodnight.

Night fell in love with her at first glance, and leapt onto the t-shirt she wears to bed—you know that really tight one that doesn't really cover her ass, and when she wears **those white cotton**—never mind. So, he jumped on her. Lucky you, right?
Well not lucky me.

Because Night knows that I'm his *competition.* After riding into bed with your mom last night, he waited until she was asleep, and then woke me by **tapping on my fucking eyeball**. He crawled across my face and started telling me all this about how *he* was going to take over as *the man of the house*, starting by taking over my duties in bed, and before I even knew what the fuck was happening, **he did this:**

Now, I'm only taking down my shorts to show you what Night did to me. It's *terrible*. It's just... know what? You don't need to see it. You can imagine what he did. And it hurts. **Oh, good gawd it hurts.**

Anyway, Night sent me in here to tell you that *he'll* be your dad from now on and if you don't like it, **he'll fucking kill you in your sleep.**

I have to try and make it to the hospital—*like it will matter.*

He's under my hat, biting the fuck out of my head right now.

I love you.

I always will.

Goodnight.

(and goodbye)

I'll end this book with some
Helpful, Happy Poems
I'm going to make up right now
Because that last story was **scary**
and I can't have you running off to
Tell Your Mom or Something

Dead Bodies in Water

They're *pruney* and they can't swim.
If they have clothes on, fish will eat the covered parts last.

Poking them makes holes.

When they wash up on shore
Things stick in their hair.
They will smell bad, even to sharks,

Unless the sea pickles them.

Kevin Shamel & Jim Agpalza

Tape

It is good to tape things.
When there is tape
It should be used for its purpose,
Not left stuck to itself in a circle.

Also, don't eat it.

Adults Rule, Kids Drool, I Win Because I'm Bigger

Being a kid is dumb for so many reasons.
You can't do so many things that adults can do.
It is *so hard* to find cigarettes, weed and beer.
And to **see boobs** or drive cars.
I guess that's it, really.

But it's still dumb to be a kid.

So Many Things

A blister on your heel will **kill you,**

And so will a sliver in that *webbing stuff* between your fingers.

So will **swallowing your snot** when you snurk it into your throat.

Pulling on a hangnail or getting two paper-cuts at one time **will kill you.**

You will die in real life if you die in a daydream, too, *just like regular dreams.*

You will die if you think about **a latex-clad monkey brandishing a straight razor** or a **hairless horse pooping on a plate.** Oh, shit, did you just think about those things?

Farting and burping at the same time **will kill you.**

Being wakened while sleepwalking **will kill you.**

Biting your tongue while you're eating pizza **will kill you** (it doesn't matter what kind of pizza).

Hitting two of your funny bones at once **will kill you,** And so will hiccupping and hitting just one funny bone at the same time.

You will die if you spin around in a circle **68 times**.

Sipping from a cup of hot chocolate that has gone cold **will kill you.**

Eating two different kinds of donuts together will kill you (unless you drink coffee, which kids do not because if they did, **IT WOULD KILL THEM!)**

You will die if you don't read this poem ten times **right now.**

Jim Agpalza is a freelance artist who has done cover art and illustrations for various bizarro presses.

He was born and raised on a tiny, steamy island in the middle of the Pacific Ocean where the tropical heat affected his mind/loins and art enough to make him move to the Pacific Northwest where he now resides with his wife, two kids, and his...ghost cat.

In his spare time he likes to train his son in the ancient art of pronouncing the letter "L" with the letter "W".

Kevin Shamel is an elusive character who spends his time bouncing from the future to the past and generally mucking up what day it is on whichever side of the equator he finds himself.

He has written several books, but none that have strictly warned against allowing children to read them (though he likely should have done so before now).

He DOES have children. No one is sure how smart it was of him to do that, but it is done.

Slub Glub in the Weird World of the Weeping Willows— Andrew Goldfarb

A creepy cute, voodoo cartoon set in a world of ghouls, witches, and pink monkeys. Slub Glub (a blue glob-like creature) has awoken to find his world has been flooded by the tears of the Weeping Willows. His quest to help cure the sadness of the willows leads him on an interplanetary adventure that will reveal the secret meaning of the world.

Alongside the beautiful weeping Willowmina, he will encounter raccoon bandits, hyena-riding witches, a Baron who controls ghosts, Seamort the giant squid, and finally Lump-Lump, the Omnipotent Master of All Reality disguised as a beach bum. Like a more twisted Jim Henson or a rockabilly Tim Burton, this is a brilliantly surreal tale for children of all ages and a perfect introduction to the weird world of musician/artist/author Andrew Goldfarb.

The Faggiest Vampire — Carlton Mellick III

Deep in The Land of Broodsarrow, just outside the village of Gneirwil, and high on a cliff overlooking the Everbleed Sea, there stands the faggiest gothic castle that any mortal being has ever seen. Living in this ancient faggy castle is none other than the well-renowned vampire, Dargoth Van Gloomfang. The citizenry of Broodsarrow sure has its share of faggy vampires, but old Dargoth has always been by far the faggiest of them all.

That is, until a new vampire came to town. A younger, hippper vampire. One that emits such a grand amount of fagginess that one cannot help but be completely overwhelmed by his presence. Now Dargoth Van Gloomfang must figure out a way to out-shine this young newcomer if he wishes to ever reclaim his throne as . . . the faggiest vampire.

MachoPoni: A Prance with Death—Lotus Rose

From the author of Malice in Wonderland. In the first volume of the epic Poniworld Chronicles, MachoPoni has no choice but to enter the Dark Kingdom, where the undead ponies roam. He must rescue Dust, the poni he loves from the dark princess's castle, using wit, creativity and his magic bouncy blue ball to survive. A twisted parody of My Little Pony, The Care Bears, and other 80's staples.

Other Books by
Kevin Shamel
from
Eraserhead Press
Bigfoot Cop

He's huge. He's hairy. He's pissed off and he's got a badge. He's Bigfoot Cop. Bigfoot is a renegade detective on the edge. He's no longer the tranquil solitary creature of legend; he's now a foot-stomping, car-flipping crime fighter who can't stop ripping everyone's fucking arms off when he gets mad. After he destroys an entire city block while trying to apprehend a group of petty criminals, the police chief transfers him to Missing Persons and assigns him a new partner he doesn't want— Lyle Straits, a crotchety by-the-book detective who is allergic to animal dander. The unlikely duo is tasked with solving the rising number of local disappearances (mostly redheads). But what starts as a routine investigation turns into the biggest case the world has ever seen.

Island of the Super People

"A completely
original take on the
super hero genre."
- Carlton Mellick III

Four students and their anthropology professor journey to a remote island to study its indigenous population. But this is no ordinary native culture.

They're super heroes and villains with flesh costumes and outlandish abilities like self-detonation, musical eyelashes, microwave hands, whalemancing, super boobs, and the power to turn anything into fuzzy pink bunnies.

When evil government forces threaten the island, the students and super people must join together to fight. Only through their combined powers can they save themselves from total destruction.

Rotten Little Animals

ANIMALS ARE PEOPLE, TOO!

And that is messed up. So they have independent cinema. See what happens when an animal film crew kidnap a human boy and make a movie of the abduction. Read things about Nature that just aren't natural. Fear your pets from this day forward. With zombie-cat attacks, gun-blasting massacres, drugged-out puppet shows, exploding car chases, camera-chickens, bat acrobats, wild sex, martini parties and torture-ROTTEN LITTLE ANIMALS is a crazy ride through the underground animal film scene and on to the Big Time.

Find **these books** and
more at **Amazon.com**

and other fine *purveyors* of
bizarro books

from **Eraserhead Press!**